There's a Weasel Behind My Easel!

Oh! What Shall I Do?

BY

TIFFANY WHEAT

AuthorHouse™
1663 Liberty Drive
Bloomington, IN 47403
www.authorhouse.com
Phone: 1 (800) 839-8640

Published by AuthorHouse 08/10/2018

ISBN: 978-1-5462-5477-5 (sc)
ISBN: 978-1-5462-5476-8 (e)

Library of Congress Control Number: 2018909346

Print information available on the last page.

This book is printed on acid-free paper.

authorHOUSE®

There's a Weasel behind My Easel!

Oh! What Shall I Do?

By Tiffany Wheat

Once upon a long time ago, I met her-a gorgeous gluten-free baker named Greta, whose real name was Georgetta. Greta had just figured out what mysterious guest had been eating everything in her garden including her poinsettia, while playing rock-paper-scissors with her best friend, Henrietta.

Greta was so sweet but intolerant to wheat. She loved to make tasty gluten-free treats with her new cookie sheet.

Greta grabbed some eggs, vanilla, and sugar and began to bake some flourless cookies that she and her friend George the Gopher were excited to eat at the beginning of the week.

Now, right when Greta was about to live happily ever after, snacking on macaroons while watching cartoons and licking frosting off baking spoons, in crept Warren the Weasel. That afternoon he was shouting, "There's a mouse in your house!"

Greta looked at George and said, "There's a mouse in my house ready to pounce. Oh! What will we do? What will we do? Boo-hoo!"

Warren the Weasel said, "I have a suggestion! Grab a mixing bowl with a spout, and make some peanut butter cookies for that ol' mouse. She'll love every ounce and go home to her spouse."

So Greta threw on her apron and baked like she was in a race. But that ol' mouse did not come out of its safe place. So Warren ate those cookies with great haste. He didn't let a crumb go to waste. I think he even ate my grandma's china plate.

In a nearby hole lived Greta's friend Jake the Garden Snake who always loved Greta's insect cakes. He told Greta to stand on a rake and pretend to skate. Then she should bake some crab cakes, and that mouse would leave the state.

But that ol' mouse still didn't leave Greta's house. Greta said, "There's a mouse who won't leave my house-not even for her new spouse! Boo-hoo!"

Then at that very moment, Greta, who was so sweet but intolerant to wheat, had to sneeze. Warren yelled, "Freeze and roll up your sleeves and make her some gluten-free mac and cheese. It will be sure to please." Greta grabbed her measuring cups and filled them with ease while reading through her recipes.

Greta pulled out a pan from her oven made of brick. Yet another day, the mouse did not fall for Warren's trick. This made Greta, who was so sweet but intolerant of wheat, start to feel very weak.

Fueled with buckwheat flour and grief, Greta called her dear friend William the Wonderful Bookworm. He was in the kitchen, sporting his new perm, seeming quite concerned, and trying to come to terms without sounding so stern.

Now, everyone knew William was a big sap. So he asked Benny the Beatboxing Bunny to come by and bust a funky rap. But first William wanted to know why Greta was trying to set this trap.

So Greta explained everything that had happened this week—especially how Warren had her make various delectable gluten-free treats that didn't reek like Grandma's stinky feet and how Benny's rap was offbeat.

Then out of nowhere, William said, "Why don't you go by the hole that says Maria the Miraculous Mouse and say 'hi'? Take your new friend George too; he's a nice guy. Just say, 'Hola, senorita,' and offer her some pie. It's worth a try."

So Greta asked, "Maria the Miraculous Mouse, why won't you leave my house and join your new spouse? Is he a big louse? Or are you both waiting to pounce?"

Maria the Miraculous Mouse replied, "No, not at all. It's because of that weasel behind your easel who recently caught the measles from Bertha Beetle while riding on the back of a diesel."

Maria explained how the weasel was a big sneak who was trying to steal her squeak. Greta thought, *Oh boy! He is a real creep.* So they all came up with a plan to make him lunchmeat in Henrietta's beak.

And so Greta sent an e-mail to Henrietta the Helper Hawk and asked if she would help them pull off a coup and give that weasel what he was due so that Maria wouldn't feel so blue-especially since everything she said about Warren was true.

So Greta made a fresh plate of Strout, and without a doubt out popped Warren before they could even begin to count. Maybe now Maria could finally get out.

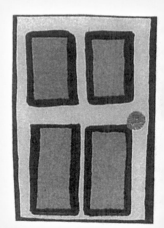

Henrietta swooped down by Greta's kitchen sink, snatched Warren in her beak, and dropped him off by grandma's stinky feet that will reek for a week.

After that, as the story goes, they all lived happily ever after Greta the Gorgeous Gluten-Free Baker, George the Gulping Gopher, and Maria the Miraculous Mouse were as grateful as could be, with their hearts filled with glee. Well everyone, but Warren whose house was next to grandma's stinky feet.

Lightning Source UK Ltd.
Milton Keynes UK
UKHW02f0728040918
328262UK00006B/105/P